Chapter One

This is a story about my uncle and aunt. And guess what? They're both called Pat!

Last year, Mum and Dad agreed I'd stay with Uncle-and-Auntie Pat during the summer holidays.

Uncle-and-Auntie Pat live at Wishing Well Farm, way out of town. It isn't an easy place to find. Dad must have driven straight past without realising.

Before long, we were completely lost, and had to ask the way.

We followed the man's long list of directions. We drove through one village...

...and then another...

...over two bridges...

...past a huge out-of-town superstore...

...and down a twisty lane.

Finally we spotted a half-hidden broken sign.

We drove up a muddy track, and found Uncle-and-Auntie Pat feeding the animals.

'You managed to find us, then,' said Uncle Pat.
'Only *just!*' muttered Dad.

Everyone greeted each other, and then just as quickly, Mum and Dad were saying their goodbyes.

I stood and waved as their car disappeared down the dirt track.

Chapter Two

Uncle-and-Auntie Pat soon made me feel at home. They cooked me a slap-up meal – heaps of scrambled egg, jacket potatoes and fresh vegetables followed by strawberries and cream.

Then they told me about
Wishing Well Farm.

There's a farm shop...
OPEN
...an orchard...
...some fields for growing veg...
...and, of course, a very old WISHING WELL!

They showed me to my room, up in the attic. I had a great view of the farmyard.

I couldn't help noticing that the farm shop was very quiet. In fact, I didn't see a single customer all day.

That evening, when I came down to say goodnight, I overheard Uncle Pat talking with Auntie Pat.
They both looked glum as they pored over their accounts.

I felt sad, but I slept soundly that night, and lost myself in dreams of the old wishing well.

Chapter Three

In the morning, I was still thinking about the well.

'Uncle Pat, does the wishing well really work?' I asked.

Uncle Pat chuckled.

'How old is it then?' I asked.

'Older than the farm and that's over three hundred years old,' replied Auntie Pat.

'Wow!' I exclaimed. 'Have you ever tried making a wish?'
They both burst out laughing.

I knew Uncle-and-Auntie Pat hadn't money to spare, but I still had some of last week's pocket money.

I reached in my jeans. There it was – a shiny ten pence piece.

I went outside to the well. It looked rather tatty, but I tried to convince myself it *could* be magical.

I took my ten pence coin and tossed it in...

After a few seconds, I heard it splash into the water deep below.

I spent the rest of the day helping out on the farm. I fed the geese, I picked some fruit and I dug up some potatoes.

It was hard work. How I wished my wish would start working.

That night I fell asleep the moment my head touched the pillow. I had some magical dreams...

I dreamt the geese laid golden eggs.

I dreamt the fruit trees grew five pound notes.

And I dreamt I dug up some buried treasure along with the potatoes!

But in the morning when I woke up, I realised they were only dreams.

Chapter Four

The following day, it was scrambled eggs again!

It's just as well I love eggs. But I did begin to wonder if the wishing well genie had heard my wish.

After breakfast, I helped tidy up the shop. Things were as quiet as ever.

I decided to have a word with the wishing well genie.

'I'm still waiting for my wish to come true,' I whispered.

Then a thought came to me: if the genie was at the bottom of the well, he might not be able to hear me. Maybe I should talk a little louder. Or a lot louder.

I decided I might as well shout!

'Give me a sign, give me a sign,' the wishing well echoed.

'That's it!' I thought.

I ran to give Uncle-and-Auntie Pat the message.

'He could be right,' said Auntie Pat.

‘You need a *new* sign,’ I said. ‘So that motorists don’t just whizz by.’
Uncle Pat scratched his head.
‘I suppose it’s worth a try,’ he said at last.

So we got to work.

We didn't stop at making just one sign.

We made lots and lots and lots.

It took us all afternoon to put up the signs. They looked great.

No one could miss Wishing Well Farm now!

Chapter Five

The next day, business began to pick up. Not dramatically, but bit by bit.

A sack of potatoes here...

...and a punnet of strawberries there.

At one time we actually had three customers in the shop at once. That must have been a record!

By the next week, things were even better. Word had spread about Wishing Well Farm.

Uncle-and-Auntie Pat weren't likely to become millionaires, but business was better than it had been for years.

Chapter Six

My stay at Wishing Well Farm couldn't last forever, and one afternoon I spotted Dad's car in the queue of vehicles in the farmyard.

It was great to see Mum and Dad again.

I showed them round the farm.

'And last but not least, this is the famous wishing well,' I told them.

They both laughed out loud. Maybe it *was* just a silly old legend after all.

I went and packed my bag whilst the others had a cup of tea. Then I said my goodbyes to Uncle-and-Auntie Pat.

I decided to visit the wishing well one last time. Just in case there *was* a genie, I shouted 'goodbye' really loudly.

'Goodbye, goodbye...' he shouted back. 'It's been nice meeting you...'

The End